I0640818

Charles Walter Brown

Nathan Hale, the Martyr Spy

Charles Walter Brown

Nathan Hale, the Martyr Spy

ISBN/EAN: 9783337297732

Printed in Europe, USA, Canada, Australia, Japan

Cover: Foto ©Raphael Reischuk / pixelio.de

More available books at **www.hansebooks.com**

NATHAN HALE

THE MARTYR SPY.

An Incident of the Revolution.

BY

CHARLES W. BROWN.

"I wish to be useful. If the exigencies of my country demand a peculiar service, its claims to the performance of that service are imperious."—NATHAN HALE.

———

ILLUSTRATED.

———

THE SUNNYSIDE SERIES. No. 107. July, 1899. Issued Quarterly. $1.00 per year. Entered at New York Post-Office as second-class matter. (COPYRIGHT 1899, BY J. S. OGILVIE PUBLISHING COMPANY.)

———

NEW YORK:
J. S. OGILVIE PUBLISHING COMPANY,
57 ROSE STREET.

TO

THE SONS AND DAUGHTERS

OF THE

AMERICAN REVOLUTION

THIS WORK IS RESPECTFULLY DEDICATED BY

THE AUTHOR.

CONTENTS.

NATHAN HALE,

THE MARTYR SPY.

PRELIMINARY CHAPTER.

In the fall of 1868 there appeared in a Newark, New Jersey, paper the following interview reminiscent of the scenes and incidents of the stirring days of Washington. The author has taken the liberty to expunge all that does not relate to the Revolution and the two most dramatic incidents that occurred during the formative period of American independence. In addition there have been merged into one account parts of an earlier interview, extracts from private papers, and additional memoranda. But in this narration the author reproduces the thought and style of Captain Daniel Thurston Wandell, his maternal great grandfather:

"I was born at Newburg, Orange County, New York, the 22d day of October, 1770, and am to-day ninety-eight years of age. My father served seven years during the Revolution in Colonel Malcomb's Second New York Artillery. From 1794 to 1828 my business was on the water, most of the time as captain of a coasting sloop. I was employed by the government in 1812 to transport am-munition and troops on the waters about New York, Baltimore and Philadelphia.

"I recollect well the scenes connected with the capture, the execution and the burial of Major John André, eighty-eight years ago the 2d of the present month on Mabie's farm at Tappan. Yes, I have a faint recollection of the execution of Nathan Hale also, though I was but six years old at the time. He was hung in New York City, which was sixty miles down the Hudson from where I was then living. On the day following the evacuation of New York by the British I went down to New York with my father. This was on the 26th of November, 1783, seven years after the execution of Captain Hale. My father took me out to the old Beekman homestead, which was General Howe's headquarters during the greater period of the occupation of the city by the British, but was then, as it had been for the past six months, occupied by General Carleton. From there we went over to Colonel Rutger's orchard, which we found crowded with patriotic and loyal citizens desirous of paying their respects to the memory of Captain Nathan Hale. For seven years the city was occupied by the British army and no one was permitted to enter without the necessary papers, or under a flag of truce, and then only under escort. This being the first day following the evacuation, many thousands flocked to

New York to see the changes that had taken place since the city was destroyed by fire the night preceding Hale's execution, and I presume three-fourths of the people that came to New York that day saw the tree on which Captain Hale died the year of the Declaration.

"The orchard had been well kept by the British, for it was in full bearing in the summer of 1783. I was given two apples by one of Colonel Rutger's slaves, which he said had grown on the tree on which Captain Hale was hung. The old darky was a witness to the execution, and with a cane he carried, touched the limb from which he said the rope was suspended. I was thirteen years old at the time; consequently I have a vivid recollection of the orchard, the tree, the limb, and in my mind I can picture the exact spot where the body of Nathan Hale now rests, for he was buried but a few feet from the tree on which he died. After the lapse of eighty-five years, and the marvelous growth of the city, I would be unable to locate the grave nearer than to say that it was in the vicinity of the present northwest corner of Pike and Monroe streets.

"The importance of Captain Hale's mission among the British, and his capture and execution caused great sorrow and indignation everywhere. But speaking of André, whose execution at the hands of the Americans occurred four years after Hale's death: he was imprisoned in the old Dutch Church in the village of Tappan which was half in New York and half in New Jersey. The gallows was erected about a quarter of a mile from the church. André, at his own request, walked to the gallows, being escorted by a few hundred Pennsylvania troops, his coffin at the time being taken in a cart. The gallows stood about two hundred yards from the main road, and within a few feet of a white oak tree, under which the remains were buried. Being familiar with the execution and burial of André, having witnessed both, I was called upon and tendered fifty dollars by the authorized agents of the British government to point out the grave, as they proposed, they said, to disinter the remains and remove them to England. It is needless for me to say that I refused their offer, though the amount was afterward raised to one hundred dollars. The grave was fenced in with a rail fence, as the remainder of the field was cultivated. I planted and hoed corn in the adjoining field in my younger days, and had assisted in putting in the crop that was ripening at the time André was hung.

"It was about this time that I first saw the great Washington reviewing the Pennsylvania troops stationed at this place (Tappan). General Washington reviewed these troops by walking up and

down the line, hat in hand and alone.
His hair was powdered. His vest was of
buff cloth and he wore knee breeches
with white-top boots. His coat was dark
blue with yellow fringe and lace trim-
mings, and he wore ruffles. I removed
to Baltimore in 1788, and while living
there I frequently saw Washington and
Lady Washington ride by in their chaise.
In 1792 I had the honor of voting for
General Washington for president, and
have voted at every presidential election
since. Should my life be spared to vote
for General Grant, my first and last votes
will be for two great captains—Washington and Grant.

"DANIEL THURSTON WANDELL."

For more than half a century Captain
Wandell was one of Newark's most
highly esteemd citizens, and though he
has been dead a quarter of a century, he
lived long enough to realize his desire to

vote for President Grant and in doing so the period of his life overlapped the generations from Nathan Hale to the present. His vivid recollections of the stirring days of the Revolution and the constructive period that followed; his intense patriotism and loyalty to "Old Glory," which was born June 14, 1777, have given inspiration in the preparation of this work. It has been a source of both pleasure and profit to refer to him as well as to many other published and written incidents of the Revolution coming under the observation of one in whom the author placed implicit confidence as to truth and accuracy. He regrets exceedingly that Captain Wandell did not speak further concerning the capture and excution of Nathan Hale, now that he is about to send forth a brief story of the martyr.

Our ancestral struggle for freedom— freedom of speech, of thought, of action, and form of government, is worthy of our highest consideration, and this attempt to perpetuate the devotion of one of the martyrs of the republic is sent forth with the earnest hope that it may do something toward emphasizing the importance of the cause for which our national heroes yielded up their lives. May it be read sympathetically, with charity for its defects, with appreciation of whatever excellence it may possess.

The reader is left to peruse the following chapters with a perfect assurance that along with fiction there is combined history, with its four integral parts— romance, annal, biography and memoir.

CHARLES W. BROWN.

CHICAGO, July 1, 1899.

CHAPTER II.

"POSSESSING GENIUS, TASTE AND ORDER, HE
BECAME DISTINGUISHED AS A SCHOLAR."

TWENTY-TWO miles east of Hartford,
Connecticut, in the picturesque County of
Toland, the traveler is shown a pleasant
dwelling, which he is told was erected
more than a century and a half ago.
Through the long lapse of time the foun-
dation alone has remained intact; repairs
and the remodeling necessary to render
the old dwelling habitable have left little
of the original house to be seen to-day.
The general style of colonial architec-
ture and the air of refinement, still to be
seen all through the New England country, gives the old house and its surroundings an appearance of thrift and comfort

which must have prevailed there in other days.

This was the Hale homestead. It stood upon a pleasant elevation, picturesque almost beyond description, and surrounded by a primeval forest of oak and walnut. A low stone wall, completely covered with ivy, Virginia creeper and wild rose, inclosed the roomy dwelling and its ample lawns, gardens and orchard—a typical New England home, an abode of peace, contentment, security and faith.

Stretching away in all directions, the quiet forests, wrapped in a mantle of fresh color, with here and there fields of waving corn and fragrant buckwheat, which relieved the sameness of the wooded uplands, rejoiced with all nature that this spot and this hour would be made memorable in the annals of our country. On the 6th of June, 1755, the surrounding landscape must have presented a more beautiful aspect than ever before. Let us believe that God smiled approvingly upon the young babe that came to Richard and Elizabeth Hale on that bright morning so long ago, for they were godly people and revered the Bible ''as the voice of God and the observance of the Sabbath as a binding obligation, and family worship and grace before meals as imperative duties and precious obligations.''

Early in life Richard Hale, the father of Nathan, had come from Newberry, Massachusetts, and settled near Coventry in the county of Toland. Here he married Elizabeth Strong, who we are told was a charming maiden of some eighteen years, and who had been brought up in the strictest Puritan faith. To them were born twelve children, the sixth being a boy whose young life was at times despaired of, and there was little promise of his surviving the period of in-

fancy; but with tender motherly care
and a skillful family physician, he finally
struggled through to his second year,
when he began to develop, mentally and
physically, into a robust youth.

When yet a mere child he was fond of
outdoor sports. He was a fine marks-
man, was fond of fishing in summer and
skating in winter, and was the swiftest
runner and best jumper in Toland County.
We are told that it was his delight to
place a number of sugar hogsheads, as
many as twelve, in a line and with apparent ease spring from one into the
other, and so on through them all without resting or touching his hands to the
barrels. Many other stories of his skill
as an athlete could be related, but it is
sufficient to say that whether in sport or
work he was always first among his
comrades.

Inheriting from his parents a strict
sense of religious obligation after the

manner of Puritan faith, he likewise inherited a thirst and aptitude for knowledge. His early piety, and the desire of his father to have at least one of his sons enter the ministry, suggested the wisdom of preparing Nathan for this profession. The pastor of the parish church where he had been christened, Dr. Huntington, one of the most learned and eminent Congregational divines and scholars of his time, undertook the pleasant and profitable task of directing his studies and religious training. We know with perfect assurance that Nathan proved an apt and obedient pupil, for at the youthful age of sixteen years and two months he passed the entrance examination to Yale College, being one of the youngest students if not the very youngest that ever entered that famous college.

There were but sixty students at Yale the winter of 1771 when Nathan entered, but when he graduated with the highest honors of his class in September, 1773, there were eighty-four. The thoroughness of Dr. Huntington's teaching and the excellence of Hale's scholarship displayed all through his stay at Yale, was apparent from the fact that accompanying his certificate of graduation was a statement from each of his teachers, among them one from Dr. Timothy Dwight, who was afterward .president of Yale College, that Nathan Hale was not only the youngest but one of the very best students that ever graduated from Yale College, as shown by the class records. This must have been very encouraging as well as gratifying to the young student, for it was just two years and eighteen days from the time of his entrance until his graduation at the head of his class—a record that perhaps has never since been equalled at that great university.

In addition to his brilliancy of intellect, magnificent physique and skill as an athlete, he was one of the most popular students that had ever attended Yale College. He was loved and respected by all the students and tutors alike, and though averse to giving much of his time while he was at college to social affairs, still his great popularity and affable disposition made his presence desirable at every social gathering, and he was always a welcome guest at the homes of the best families in New Haven. Dr. Lossing tells us that in 1848 he visited New Haven and stopped at the home of the venerable Eneas Munson, M.D., who had been a surgeon in the War of Independence. Dr. Munson knew Hale well during the latter period of his life at Yale College, for he was a frequent visitor at the home of Dr. Munson's father. "I was greatly impressed," said Dr. Munson, "with Hale's scientific knowledge, evinced during his conversation with my father. I am sure he was the equal of André in solid acquirements, and his taste for art and talents as an artist were quite remarkable. His personal appearance was as notable. He was almost six feet in height, perfectly proportioned, and in figure and deportment he was the most manly man I ever met. His chest was broad, his muscles were firm; his face wore a most benign expression; his complexion was roseate; his hair was soft and light brown in color, while his speech was rather low, sweet and musical. His personal beauty and grace of manner were most charming. Why, all the girls in New Haven fell in love with him and wept bitterly when they heard of his sad fate. In dress he was always neat; he was quick to lend a helping hand to a being in distress—brute or human; was always overflowing with good humor and was the idol of all of his acquaintances.''

This account of the appearance of Nathan Hale by one who knew him personally is the only authentic one extant. From this graphic description it has been possible to produce his image in stone, on canvas and in bronze. No picture is in existence, and so far as has been ascertained, but one was ever taken, and this was lost shortly after the death of its owner. The illustrations usually given and the ones used in this book, together with the busts and statues erected to his memory, were drawn from the description given by Dr. Munson, the style of dress and the manner of wearing the hair being peculiar to the period in which he lived.

Dr. Jared Sparks, who knew several of Nathan's intimate friends, among whom was Alice Adams to whom Nathan was engaged, said of him: "*Possessing genius,*

taste and order, he became distinguished
as a scholar; endowed in an eminent de-
gree with those graces and gifts of nature
which add a charm to youthful excellence, he gained universal esteem and
confidence. To high moral worth and
irreproachable character were joined
gentleness of manner, an ingenuous disposition and vigor of understanding.
No young man of his years put forth a
fairer promise of future usefulness and
celebrity; the fortunes of none were
fostered more sincerely by the generous
good wishes of his associates and the
hopes and the encouraging presages of
his superiors."

While at Yale College, Nathan Hale
was instrumental in founding the Lino-
nian Society, becoming its first president. At its anniversary in 1853 Mr.
Francis M. Finch read the following
beautiful lines in allusion to the martyr:

"To drumbeat and heartbeat,
    A soldier marches by;
There is color in his cheek,
    There is courage in his eye,
Yet to drumbeat and heartbeat
    In a moment he must die.

"By starlight and moonlight
    He seeks the Briton's camp;
He hears the rustling flag
    And the armed sentry's tramp;
And the starlight and moonlight
    His silent wanderings' lamp.

"With slow tread and still tread
    He scans the tented line;
And counts the battery guns
    By the gaunt and shadowy pine;
And his slow tread and still tread
    Gives no warning sign.

"With calm brow, steady brow,
    He listens to his doom.
In his look there is no fear

Nor a shadow trace of gloom;
But with calm brow and steady brow,
He robes him for the tomb.

"In the long night, the still night,
He kneels upon the sod;
And the brutal guards withhold
E'en the solemn Word of God!
In the long night, the still night,
He walks where Christ hath trod.

" 'Neath the blue morn, the sunny morn,
He dies upon the tree;
And mourns that he can lose
But one life for Liberty;
And the blue morn, the sunny morn,
His spirit wings are free.

"From Fame leaf and Angel leaf
From monument and urn,
The sad of Earth, the glad of Heaven,
His tragic fate shall learn;
And on Fame leaf and Angel leaf
The name of HALE shall burn!"

CHAPTER III.

"LET US ORGANIZE AND DRILL AS WE MARCH,
AND NEVER LAY DOWN OUR ARMS UNTIL
WE HAVE OBTAINED OUR INDEPENDENCE."

EAST HADDAM, Connecticut, stands on
the left bank of the Connecticut River
just below the mouth of the Salmon in
the County of Middlesex. Here came
Nathan Hale to teach his first school the
winter following his graduation from Yale
College. This was a "select" or private
school, for there were no public schools
in those days. East Haddam was then
a place of some importance and considerable wealth, and it is not surprising
that he should have had "nearly thirty
pupils of all ages, half being Latiners,"
as he wrote in his diary.

His ability and talents as a schoolmaster attracted wide attention, and before the close of the first year he received many calls to take charge of
schools in various parts of Connecticut;
one coming from Newberry, Massachusetts, where his father was born; but
the one that suited him best, perhaps because it was the home of Alice
Adams, was New London. The proprietors of the Union Grammar School of
that place offered him the preceptorship
of their school, which Hale accepted in
the following language:

"GENTLEMEN:
"I am pleased to acknowledge the re-
ceipt of your letter which came by recent
post, and will not delay longer in coming
to a decision as to which school I will
keep next term. I will agree to abide by
your agreement and terms, and will go
to New London within a fortnight to
make plans for the conduct of the
school.   NATHAN HALE."

The Union Grammar School was an institution of high grade for that period; it was designed by its proprietors to afford facilities for a thoroughly English education and the classical preparation necessary for entering college. Having but recently graduated from Yale, it was a wise choice in selecting young Hale to become its first teacher in its widened scope, and at the same time it was a high compliment to Hale's ability for one so young and with but one year's experience as a teacher. When he accepted the appointment in April, 1774, he was barely nineteen years of age. "No one could teach in this school," says an early chronicler, "but those whose character would bear the strictest scrutiny, and where Latin, English, writing and arithmetic were taught, and where the salary was seventy pounds ($350) a year, with the privilege of teaching private classes out of the regular school hours."

In a letter to his friend, Roger Alden, a classmate at Yale and afterward an adjutant in the Continental army, Hale wrote concerning his school at New London:

"NEW LONDON, May 2, 1774
"I am at present in a school in New London. I think my situation somewhat preferable to what it was last winter. My school is by no means difficult to take care of—it consists of about thirty scholars, ten of whom are Latiners, and all but one of the rest are writers. I have a very convenient schoolhouse, and the people are kind and sociable. I promise myself some more satisfaction in writing and receiving letters from you than I have as yet had.
"NATHAN HALE."

Colonel Samuel Green, of Hartford, Connecticut, who died in 1862, was one of Hale's pupils at the grammar school, and a short time before his death he said: "Nathan Hale was a man peculiarly engaging in his manners—these were mild and genteel. The scholars, old and young, were attached to him. They loved him for his tact and amiability. He was wholly without severity, and had a wonderful control over boys." This testimony agrees with many others, so it is not to be wondered at that men would follow wherever he led, whether on the march or on one of his thrilling exploits.

Hale was much given to throwing his thoughts into rhyme, and more especially while teaching at New London, for his life in the army was too active to indulge in such peaceful moods. He had one friend—William Tallmage—a classmate at Yale, whom we shall read of in a subsequent chapter as one of the captors of André, to whom Hale wrote regularly, not infrequently resorting to rhyme as the "only way of expressing one's thoughts in tenderest emotion."

His life at New London was indeed a

UNION GRAMMAR SCHOOL, NEW LONDON, CONN., WHERE
NATHAN HALE TAUGHT.

busy one. An entry in his diary preserved in the parish church at Coventry, reads: "A man ought never to lose a moment's time; if he put off a thing from one minute to the next, his reluctance is but increased." Every body in and about New London became attached to him. For a year his life was an uneventful one; he pursued his studies, taught his daily classes, conducted a class of young men and young women in Bible study on Sunday, and continued his social visitations with scrupulous regularity. His life was not such a busy one, however, but that he found time for the little romances of life. While teaching the Union Grammar School he had for one of his pupils Alice Adams, a bright, intelligent girl of sixteen years, said by some authorities to have been his stepsister and by others an adopted sister. She was a native of Canterbury, Connecticut, and was distinguished for her beauty and refinement.

An attachment sprang up between them which resulted in an engagement, the fulfillment of which depended upon the fortunes of war. "As soon as our beloved country is free from accursed British rule and the last redcoat has been driven from our shores, I will return to keep my promise." Thus spoke Nathan to Alice when he had fully made up his mind to enlist in the Continental army. In subsequent pages we shall read of her devotion and the part she played in this thrilling life-drama enacted so long ago.

The war trumpet had not yet sounded, though preparations had been in progress for many months. Old guns and pistols, swords and knives, were put in readiness to be used upon an instant's notice. Hunting was neglected for the drill and target practice. Even business was neglected, for in the shops and on the street corners, wherever men gathered, the sole topic of conversation was "war, cruel, relentless war, as the only means of obtaining our independence." At the grammar school, Hale formed the boys into a company which he drilled during intermissions and on Saturdays, using a written copy of the "manual of arms," obtained from his father who had copied it years before from an old British manual, owned by a relative in Newberry, Massachusetts. No attempt was made to conceal this warlike spirit among the boys of New London; in fact it was becoming epidemic, and it was not long until the contagion spread throughout the colonies. Even the old men, and the boys and girls, too young to realize its meaning, watched the maneuvers of the grammar school boys on the village green with pride and satisfaction.

There were no railroads, steamboats, telegraphs or telephones in those days, and it was some time before news from

New York or Boston reached the interior towns and even those along the Sound. Everybody knew, though, that the British were landing on our shores, and massing troops in Canada, New Brunswick and Nova Scotia; but aside from putting down local disturbances in a few of the coast cities, and the warlike preparations such as displayed at the grammar school, there was little to foretell the long and bloody War of Independence, "the eight years' struggle," that was soon to involve the two and three-quarters million Americans and make every boy a man and every man a patriot, until late in the afternoon of April 21, 1775, when a messenger, riding from Boston to New York, stopped at New London long enough to tell of the wonderful ride of Paul Revere and the fights at Lexington and Concord.

The news created great excitement in the village, and as the story spread from

house to house throughout the surrounding country, men and boys rushed to the
village to learn the truth of the report
and to offer their services—their lives if
necessary—to avenge the slaughter of
their countrymen. Long before night
the streets were filled with a crowd of
angry yet determined men. Just at sun-
set the doors of the courthouse were
thrown open and in a few moments the
building was filled with patriotic citizens, all anxious to give expression to
their feelings, and to enroll their names,
pledging their lives in the defense of
tbeir country. Patriotic speeches were
made by nearly a score of citizens, and
among them the voice of Nathan Hale,
the master of the grammar school, rang
through the open windows, out over the
heads of the gathering crowds and across
the blue waters of the Thames River.
With impassioned language and intense
earnestness he exhorted the people of

New London to take action at once. *"Let us organize and drill as we march, and never lay down our arms until we have obtained our independence,"* said Hale; and the appeal was not in vain. This is said to have been the first public demand for American independence made at the beginning of the great and final struggle.

A company was immediately formed with the name of Nathan Hale second on the roll. The next morning when the scholars assembled, he told them of his resolve, his hopes and his ambitions; he prayed with them, gave them each good advice, bade them all an affectionate farewell, and with his company marched away to Cambridge (Boston). By some it has been thought that a letter from Alice Adams brought him back to New London in May; but whatever the cause that called him home, it is a fact that in July we find him a lieutenant in a regi-

ment commanded by Colonel Charles
Webb—"raised by order of the General
Assembly for home defense, or if necessary, for the protection of the country
at large."

With Nathan Hale honor was everything. Truth and honesty were the twin
spirits that directed his every thought
and action. Immediately after being appointed lieutenant he addressed the following letter to the proprietors of the
grammar school:

"GENTLEMEN: Having received infor·
mation that a place is allotted me in the
army, and being inclined, as I hope, for
good reasons, to accept it, I am con-
strained to ask as a favor that which
scarce anything else would have induced
me to, which is, to be excused from keeping your school any longer. The year
for which I engaged will expire within a
fortnight, so that my quitting a few days
sooner, I hope, will subject you to no
great inconvenience.   NATHAN HALE.
"NEW LONDON, Friday, 27th April, 1775."

The company to which Lieutenant Hale was attached was under the immediate command of Major John Latimer, and was to be "subject to the orders of the Connecticut Council of Safety." Boston was the objective point of the British; first, owing to its proximity to Canada, Nova Scotia and other British outposts; and, secondly, because of its comparatively isolated position from the center of population, which was then south and west of New York City. Home defense was not deemed as essential as the defense of the coast cities and more especially where the enemy was likely to make its first attack; so, acting under orders from Washington, the commander-in-chief of the American army, Colonel Webb's regiment marched away to Boston late in September, 1775. After a long and desperate struggle, lasting from early autumn until late the following spring, the British and a host of Tories

IN CONGRESS

The Delegates of the United Colonies of *New-Hampshire, Massachusetts-Bay, Rhode-Island, Connecticut, New-York, New-Jersey, Pennsylvania, the Counties of Newcastle, Kent, and Sussex on Delaware, Maryland, Virginia, North-Carolina and South-Carolina* to *Nathan Hale Esq* —

WE reposing especial trust and confidence in your patriotism, valour, conduct and fidelity. DO these presents constitute and appoint you to be *Captain in the nineteenth Regiment of foot Commanded by Colonel Charles Webb* in the army of the United Colonies raised for the defence of American Liberty, and for repelling every hostile invasion thereof. You are therefore carefully and diligently to discharge the duty of *Captain* —— by doing and performing all manner of things thereunto belonging. And we do strictly charge and require all officers and soldiers under your command, to be obedient to your orders as *Captain* —— And you are to observe and follow such orders and directions from time to time as you shall receive from this or a future Congress of the United Colonies, or Committee of Congress for that purpose appointed, or Commander in Chief for the time being of the army of the United Colonies or any other your superior officer, according to the rules and discipline of war, in pursuance of the trust reposed in you. This commission to continue in force until revoked by this or a future Congress

Attest *Cha Thomson secy*

January the first 1776

'Order of the Congress.

John Hancock President

COPY OF NATHAN HALE'S COMMISSION AS CAPTAIN.

were driven out of Boston, taking refuge in Halifax. For bravery displayed in this siege Lieutenant Hale was commissioned captain by Congress, January 1, 1776.

So earnest and unselfish was Captain Hale's patriotism that when in December, 1775, a number of the men in his company, whose term of service had expired or was about to expire, determined to return home, he appealed to their patriotism, and their loyalty to their comrades whose term of enlistment was not half up; finally he offered to divide every dollar he possessed, including the month's pay he had not yet received, if they would remain until spring. Successful in this endeavor as in everything else he undertook, his patriotic utterances moved many to re-enlist. Thus to Nathan Hale is due much credit for the early expulsion of the British from Boston, for he strengthened the patriot cause in their own hearts, among their own people, and won new and powerful allies across the sea. Had the men whose terms of service were expiring not been urged, even bribed, by one in whom they had implicit confidence, there would have been such a wholesale desertion that the British would have observed the demoralized and disorganized condition in the American camp and the siege would have been maintained until reinforcements arrived and the patriot army would have been forced to retire in disgrace.

It was here that Washington became acquainted with Captain Hale and noticed his fitness to command or undertake any perilous mission intrusted to him. It was on Washington's recommendation to Congress that Hale was promoted to a captaincy, and later on we shall see how Hale repaid his commander at a time when such service as he volunteered to perform could apparently save the

army and the cause for which he staked
his life.

The following beautiful lines by William Cullen Bryant were written while
the poet was in contemplation of the sacrifice and patriotic devotion of the early
martyrs to the cause of freedom. The
character of men like Nathan Hale, if
not actually the man himself, undoubtedly moved the great poet to pen these
verses in memory of the martyrs of the
Revolution:

SEVENTY-SIX.

What heroes from the woodland sprung,
  When through the fresh-awakened
      land
The thrilling cry of freedom rung,
And to the work of warfare strung,
  The yeoman's iron hand!

Hills flung the cry to hills around,
  And ocean mart replied to mart,

And streams, whose springs were yet
    unfound
Pealed far away the startling sound,
  Into the forest's heart.

Then marched the brave from rocky
    steep,
  From mountain river swift and cold;
The borders of the stormy deep,
The vales where gathered waters sleep,
  Sent up the strong and bold.

As if the very earth again
  Grew quick with God's creating breath,
And from the sods of grove and glen,
Rose ranks of lion-hearted men
  To battle to the death.

The wife whose babe first smiled that day,
  The fair fond bride of yester eve,
And aged sire and matron gray,
Saw the loved warriors haste away,
  And deemed it sin to grieve.

Already had the strife begun;
   Already blood on Concord's plain,
Along the springing grass had run;
And blood had flowed at Lexington,
   Like brooks of April rain.

That death stain on the vernal sward,
   Hallowed to freedom all the shore;
In fragments fell the yoke abhorred—
The footsteps of a foreign lord
   Profaned the soil no more.

CHAPTER IV.

"I WILL UNDERTAKE IT!—THE SOLDIER
SHOULD NEVER CONSULT HIS FEARS
WHEN DUTY CALLS."

AFTER the expulsion of the British
from Boston, and their return from Nova
Scotia, where they had been reinforced
by six shiploads of hired Hessians, New
York became the objective point of attack. In order to protect Boston it was
necessary to maintain a large army
there, which Howe well reasoned would
lessen the American forces at New
York; then the city could by a combined attack on land and water easily be
taken. The population of New York
at this time was between twenty-
one and twenty-two thousand, some

smaller than Boston, but less than half the size of Philadelphia which remained the largest city in America until 1820. The commanding situation and comparatively open harbor and the immense grain and provision trade made the occupation of this city greatly to be desired by Lord Howe. In proportion to its population, no other city in the colonies contained so many British sympathizers as New York. Lord Howe knew this and he brought the combined strength of his army and navy to drive Washington from his seemingly well-fortified position.

In April, 1776, Captain Hale's regiment, under General Heath, reached New York by the way of Norwich, Connecticut, where it had been ordered by Washington to aid him in the defense of that city. At Norwich, Captain Hale left his regiment temporarily to organize a company of Connecticut Rangers, a corps composed of picked men from the

different Connecticut regiments to be
placed under the command of Lieutenant-Colonel Thomas Knowlton, who had
distinguished himself in the battle of
Bunker (Breed's) Hill. This company
of rangers was known as "Congress'
Own." The following month (May) Captain Hale made his way to New York to
rejoin his regiment under General Heath.
He had no sooner reached New York
than he performed a daring feat, that
made his name known to every soldier in
the Continental army.

A British sloop, laden with provisions,
a small amount of ammunition and about
thirty stand of arms, was anchored in the
East River under the protection of the
guns of the British man-of-war, *Asia*.
General Heath gave Hale permission to
attempt the capture of the supply vessel.
With a few picked men, probably from
Glover's brigade, who were chiefly sea-
men, and as resolute as himself, he pro-

ceeded in a whaleboat silently at midnight to the side of the sloop, unob-
served by the sentinel on deck. Hale
and his men sprang on board, secured
the sentinel, confined the crew below
the hatches, raised her anchor and took
her into Coenties Slip just at the dawn of
day (April 20, 1776). Captain Hale was
at the helm. The victors were greeted
with loud huzzas from a score of voices
when the sloop touched the wharf. The
provisions were distributed among Hale's
hungry fellow-soldiers, while the sloop,
ammunition and guns went to the general supply depot.

The success of the undertaking was
commended by Washington, for it not
only added to their scanty supply of provisions, arms, etc., but gave them nearly
a score of prisoners to exchange for an
even number of their men captured in the
attack upon Boston. This was but one
of more than a dozen exploits in which

Hale participated during the spring and summer of 1776. He was successful in each and had received the thanks of his commanding officer, the praises of his fellow-soldiers and promotion by a special act of Congress at the request of Washington.

There was much to be done in the vicinity of New York that year. Washington, with Generals Sullivan, Putnam and Stirling, had been busy for months planning the Long Island campaign which resulted so disastrously to the Americans. At midnight on August 28th a heavy fog rose over New York bay and hid the armies from each other. It continued throughout the entire day and night that followed. On the evening of the 29th the army silently yet quickly commenced embarking from the point now occupied by the Fulton Ferry. The boats moved noiselessly with muffled oars, and in the course of six hours and a half, the whole army, with their baggage and munitions, the artillery alone excepted, crossed in safety to New York. Washington had remained until the last company had embarked. He had not slept for forty-eight hours, so great was his anxiety to save his men and add to their comfort in every way possible.

Secure of his prey, Howe had no suspicion of what was going on under cover of one of the blackest fogs that ever settled over New York bay. Many times during the long struggle the patriot army had cause to believe that their destiny was in the keeping of Providence, but nowhere does it appear more convincing than on the day and night of August 29, 1776. With three times the number of men, and every man well drilled and well equipped, well clothed and well fed, and having just been victorious in one of the best-planned battles of the war, we do not wonder at the surprise of General

Howe when he awoke on the morning of
August 30th to find that his victory on
Long Island had not been as complete as
he thought it was on the morning of the
27th.

The British army was then thirty
thousand strong and lay in intrenched
detachments along the shores of New
York Bay and the East River, from the
present Greenwood Cemetery to Flush-
ing and beyond. The soldiers were
veterans and were flushed with recent
victories on Long Island. They were
commanded by able officers and sup-
ported by a powerful naval force of half
a hundred vessels. The entire army
was well equipped with stores, artillery
and all munitions necessary for main-
taning a long siege or for resisting a sud-
den attack on land or water.

On the other hand the American army
was in a demoralized and most perilous
condition. The soldiers were in a far

worse condition than they were the winter before. Their clothing was in rags
and they clamored in vain for pay, for
blankets, and for satisfying food. One-
third of the army, which numbered less
than eleven thousand men, were without
tents; one-fourth of them were on the
sick roll, and the few well ones were half-
starved and in rags. These were some
of the conditions our forefathers had to
face in their struggle for liberty, that we,
their descendants, might reap the reward
their lives so dearly purchased.

About this time Lord Howe was instructed by the British government to
"receive the submission of all rebels who
would throw themselves on the king's
mercy." To this Washington replied,
"The Americans are simply defending
their rights, and having committed no
faults, they need no pardon." Having failed in this offer Howe supple-
mented it by offering bounties to those

who would desert the "rebel cause."
There can be little doubt that many of
the faint-hearted and skeptical ones did
take advantage of Howe's offer, either to
desert, or to enter the British lines to
keep from starving, for it is a matter of
history that soldiers deserted by com-
panies and even by regiments. The army
was fearfully demoralized and seemed
hourly on the point of dissolution, when
Washington called a council of war, September 7th, to consider the important
questions, "What shall be done?"
"Shall we defend or abandon New
York?"

After a long and exhaustive argu-
ment, lasting far into the night, it was
decided to defend the city at all haz-
ards. Congress had urged that "care
be taken that no damage be done to the
city," and they determined to defend it
at the cost of their lives.

Washington had taken up his headquarters at the home of Robert Murray on Murray Hill, not far from the present site of the Grand Central station, New York. The British ships passed up and down both sides of Manhattan Island; scouts sent out by Washington reported great activity among the British everywhere, but they could not penetrate nor even reasonably conjecture their designs in this naval display or movements of troops across both rivers. It was of the utmost importance to know something of the enemy's real intentions and thus anticipate their movements in order to compensate for lack of numbers and munitions. Becoming desperate, Washington wrote to General Heath, then stationed at Kingsbridge, a few miles above the city: "As everything, in a manner, depends upon obtaining intelligence of the enemy's movements, I do most earnestly entreat you and General Clinton to exert yourselves to accomplish

this most desirable end. Leave no stone
unturned, nor do not stick at expense to
bring this to pass, as I was never more
uneasy than on account of my want of
knowledge on this score. Keep constant
lookout with good glasses on some commanding heights that look well on the
other shore.''

In his perplexity and desperate frame
of mind, Washington called another
council of war that same night (September 12th). He told his officers that he
could not procure the least information
concerning the intentions of the enemy,
and asked the usual questions of late:
''What shall be done?'' ''What can be
done?''

Finally the council resolved to call
for some one to volunteer to go into
the British camps on Long Island
and procure if possible the information
so eagerly sought by Washington. It
needed one skilled in military and

scientific knowledge; a good draughtsman, one with quick eye, unflinching
courage and cool head; a man on
whose judgment and fidelity implicit re-
liance might be placed; one with tact,
caution and great sagacity. Was there
in all the American army a man who
possessed half of these requisites?
Washington sent for Lieutenant-Colonel
Knowlton, to whom he made known his
wishes, and asked him to seek for a
trustful man for this service either in his
own regiment or in any other in the
army. "Some one," said Washington,
"must penetrate the British camp and
lift this veil of secrecy, or the American
army is lost," and he did not hesitate to
communicate this opinion to his board
of officers.

Summoning a number of officers to a
conference at his headquarters, the next
day (September 14th) in the name of
Washington—the commander-in-chief of

the American army, Colonel Knowlton
called for a volunteer for the important
service. The officers were surprised and
did not hesitate to express themselves in
strong language at the very thought of
asking one of their number to descend to
the level of a common spy, even to accomplish so important a task as called
for by Washington. Colonel Knowlton
again pointed out to them the dire necessity of securing this important information; "for," said he, "not only the lives
and fortunes of the entire army are at
stake, but our mothers, our wives and
our children at home will fall a prey to
the desperate and licentious creatures
who mainly make up the British army in
America."

It must have been a thought of home
and of her whom he had chosen to
be his wife when this bitter strife was
over, that led Nathan Hale, pale and
weak from the effects of a recent illness

brought on by exposure and the lack of proper food, to arise and in a slow, but determined voice to say:

"*I will undertake it! The soldier should never consult his fears when duty calls.*"

Mr. Stuart says that to appreciate the position of Captain Hale it is necessary to dwell a moment upon it. His was a mission, that of a spy, not only hazardous, but also ignominious. In the judgment of every civilized nation, in the eye of all national law, the use of spies is deemed "a clandestine practice and a deceit in war." It is a fraud unworthy of an open, manly enemy—scarcely redeemed in motive by any exigency of danger—and pregnant with the worst mischief in stimulating, from a fear of betrayal, the vengeance of a foe, and in undermining those sentiments of honor, which, like gleams of sunlight upon a thunder-clouded sky, tend to soften the blackness of war.

The spy is the companion of darkness. He lurks—or if he moves in the light, it is behind walls, in the shadow of trees, in the loneliness of cliffs, under the cover of hills, in the gloom of ditches, skulking with the owl, the lynx, or the Indian. Or if he enters the camp of an enemy, he insinuates himself and winds treacherously into confidence. If caught, the certain penalty is death on the gallows. When Hale arose, the gossip of the indignant officers ceased.

Astonishment was manifest on all sides, and while a few did not hesitate to appeal to Hale to retract his bold and reckless proffer, the majority of those present knew his determined nature too well to think it advisable to offer a protest. They all knew Hale intimately. They loved him, for he had a gentle disposition, a kind heart, and yet he was the bravest among his fellows. Captain William Hull, a member of Colonel

Knowlton's staff, and Hale's most intimate friend in the army, and who afterward became a general in the War of
1812, used all the persuasive power at
his command to dissuade him from his
rash and suicidal resolve. In reply, not
to lay aside the dignified and honorably
earned title and office of captain for that
of a common spy, Hale replied in tones
that grow louder as the years roll on:

"Every kind of service necessary for
the public good becomes honorable by
being necessary."

Then turning to all those assembled,
and with no more show of impatience or
excitability than he displayed in debates
at college, he said: "Gentlemen, I think I
owe to my country the accomplishment
of an object so important and so much
desired by the commander-in-chief of
her armies, and I know of no mode of obtaining the information than by assuming a disguise and passing into the ene-

my's camp. I am fully sensible of the consequences of discovery and capture in such a situation. But for a year I have been attached to the army, and have not rendered any material service, while receiving a compensation for which I make no return. Yet I am not influenced by any expectation of promotion or pecuniary reward. *I wish to be useful; every kind of service for the public good becomes honorable by being necessary. If the exigencies of my country demand a pecular service, its claims to the performance of that service are imperious.*"

To further justify his act in the eyes of his parents and those near and dear to him, he penned these brief lines to his father on the eve of his departure for Long Island: "A sense of duty urges me to sacrifice everything for my country. I am about to undertake a perilous mission into the enemy's country at the behest of my general. I leave to-night,

perhaps to return, perhaps not." Well
he knew the dangers of the undertaking
and the fate in store for him should he
be captured in territory held by the
enemy.

Notwithstanding all the aversion, par-
ticularly of soldiers, to all those who dis-
guisedly enter a military camp to bear
off its secrets to an enemy, and the in-
stantaneousness with which such per-
sons pass from capture to the gallows
—as a last resort its employment is urged
and is not judged unworthy a great commander. The exigency of the American
cause would not permit the employment
in so important an undertaking of one
not skilled as a draughtsman, unprac-
ticed in military observation, and least
of all a common mercenary, allured by
the hope of a large reward. Accurate
measurements, estimates of the number
of the enemy, their distribution, the form
and position of their various encamp-

ments, the unguarded whispers in camp
of officers or men, could not be trusted to,
much less accomplished by, the common
soldier.   Hence, when the most intelligent, most methodical, most painstaking
scholar, soldier and patriot in the American army offered himself to be sent on
so perilous a mission, his acceptance by
Washington, who knew him both as a
man and a soldier, was instantaneous;
so says an early writer.

Further effort on the part of his companions to dissuade him from the undertaking was abandoned, and, accompanied
by Colonel Knowlton and Captain Hull,
Hale appeared before General Washington at two o'clock the same afternoon to
receive in detail the instructions concerning his dangerous, though vitally
important mission.   In addition to the
general order from Washington to "ad-
mit Captain Nathan Hale without pass-
word or countersign to all friendly

camps," he also carried an order from Colonel Knowlton requesting all owners of American vessels to convey him to any point on Long Island, or anywhere else, that Hale might designate.

Leaving the camp on Harlem Heights at eight o'clock on the night of September 15th, Hale was accompanied by his trusted friends, Asher Wright and Sergeant Stephen Hempstead, members of his own company, who sought permission of Colonel Knowlton to accompany him as far as it was deemed advisable. With prayers and wishes for his safe return, Hale left his companions and friends and passed out into a night wrapped in an impenetrable fog.

CHAPTER V.

"HE FITTED ALL THE REQUIREMENTS CON-
TAINED IN WASHINGTON'S CALL FOR A
VOLUNTEER."

IN assuming the character of a schoolmaster seeking employment as a loyal-
ist disgusted with the "rebel cause,"
Hale felt that he could move among the
various camps of the British with perfect freedom and without the slightest
danger of suspicion as to his mission or
his rank in the army. He had changed
from the full regimentals of a captain in
the Continental army to the dress of
a village schoolmaster, in velvet knick-
erbockers with lace collar and cuffs
and broad-brimmed felt hat.

East River and the western end of
Long Island Sound were crowded with

British cruisers of all sizes, but farther up the Sound where it is approximately twelve miles wide, it was thought to be entirely free from British surveillance; so Hale and his companions decided to make their way to Norwalk, keeping well back from the shore to avert suspicion, should they afterward be seen over on the Island. Without any mishap they reached Norwalk at about noon September 16th. After fully explaining his proposed plans to Wright and Hempstead, Hale handed his military commission to Wright, together with other valuable papers, with instructions to give them to Captain Hull to be sent to Alice Adams should he not return. He then gave final directions to Hempstead to remain at Norwalk five days, or until September 21st, and to send a boat for him early on the morning of that day to a point across the Sound indicated by the use of a field glass. The spot where the parting took place was just south of Norwalk on Wilson's Point, and some forty miles northeast of New York City in his native State, Connecticut.

Authorities are at variance as to Hale's movements after he departed from Norwalk on the night of September 16th; but there is a unanimity of opinion as to his being taken across the Sound on the small coasting sloop Huntington, commanded by Captain Enoch Pond, and put ashore at Huntington Bay, not far from where the line separating Queens from Suffolk counties touches the Sound.

The shore line of Long Island is very irregular, especially along the Sound. For a considerable distance back from the water's edge this unevenness is softened by a dense growth of under-brush and dwarf timber; but the point designated by Hale as the most convenient and easy of approach by Hempstead, was a barren promontory of about five hundred yards shore-line, and rising less than twenty-five feet above the waters of this sheltered inlet.

About three o'clock on the morning of September 17th, he passed the tavern of Widow Rachel Chichester, called "The Cedars," but fearing his disguise so recently assumed might not be complete, he did not stop at the tavern, but went on to the farmhouse of one William Johnson, three-quarters of a mile farther, where the road crosses a small stream called Cold Creek, or Spring Run. Here he breakfasted and was given a bed, where he slept until two hours after sunrise. Before seeking the British lines he questioned Johnson as to his chances of securing their district school or one in the immediate neighborhood. He learned from Johnson that Widow Chichester, or Mother Chick, as she was familiarly called, kept the tavern at "The Cedars," which was the resort, not only of all the

Tories in the vicinity, but of the British soldiers as well.

After getting all the information he could with safety from Johnson, he made his way to the British camp, four miles south of "The Cedars." Here he mingled freely with the soldiers, learning little, however, of their movements, owing to the unsettled condition of Howe's plans. Tradition, as well as history, is silent as to Hale's movements for the next two or three days, but in the absence of any positive information we infer that he moved rapidly among the British camps from "The Cedars" to Brooklyn and back, securing the information so much desired by Washington. His risk—his watchfulness — his fatigue—his anxiety of mind—his suffering from cold—his loss of sleep—his bivouac by the rock, the fence, upon the tree or in the ditch—his stealthy noting of posts, situations, numbers, plans, by the glare of

day, or by the dim moonlight or flicker-
ing lantern—his eluding of patrols and
guards—his conciliation of camps—all
these, the particulars of that vital quest
in which Hale was engaged, we are left,
says one authority, in the dearth of any
memorials, to conjecture.

By this time Hale felt perfectly secure in his disguise and did not hesitate
to go and come at will wherever his in-
clination suggested. He knew that "The
Cedars" was the rendezvous of the British officers, and that all matters of importance would likely be discussed there; so
on the night of September 20th he went
boldly to the tavern, which he had here-
tofore avoided, to secure lodging and
breakfast. The evening was spent in
noisy carousal by the soldiers, and much
valuable information must have been
disclosed, interspersed with profane
stories and vulgar songs by the drunken
officers, for it was known that orders

had been given to "break camp and start for New York City" the following day. This information was carefully noted by Hale who, while he mingled with the officers, refused to drink, or to participate in their drunken toasts to King George.

It has been asserted, but without any positive proof, that a cousin by the name of William Hale, a rival for the hand of Alice Adams, and a staunch British sympathizer, was at the tavern that night and revealed the identity and evident purpose of Nathan Hale to the British. Whatever the facts may be, it is nevertheless true that he was not the direct cause of Hale's arrest and conviction, for on the morning of September 21, 1776, after a night spent in company with a dozen drunken officers, Hale left the tavern one hour before dawn to look for the boat he had instructed Hempstead to have in readiness for him.

He reached in safety the point on the Sound where he had first landed and where he had directed that the boat should be sent for him. To his great joy he saw a boat with several men in it, moving toward the point designated as the place where he would be waiting to be conveyed back to Norwalk and to his companions who he knew awaited his coming with great anxiety, solicitous not only for his personal safety, but for the information he alone could reveal of the purposes of the enemy.

Not doubting that it was the boat sent by Hempstead, who he expected would be the first to welcome him back to his companions, he hastened toward the beach; as the boat approached the shore, he was astonished at seeing a barge bearing a score or more of British marines. Seeing his error, he turned to escape, when a voice from the vessel called, "Surrender or die!" Turning, he saw a number of men with muskets leveled at him. Realizing how futile it would be to attempt an escape, he meekly submitted to capture and was taken on board the vessel and conveyed to the British guardship Halifax, commanded by Captain Quarne, which was anchored two miles east at Lloyd's Neck.

As has been said, Captain Hale was an accomplished scholar, well versed in Latin, mathematics and mechanical drawing. *He fitted all the requirements contained in Washington's call for a volunteer* in respect to "unflinching courage, keen intellect, ready tact and a good draughtsman." During the four days spent among the British camps, he had procured much valuable information and had made many important drawings of the position and strength of fortifications, arms and all munitions, accouterments, etc. He had taken the precaution to wear inner soles in his shoes and beneath these he placed all the drawings with dimensions and descriptions in Latin and algebraic characters, executed on very thin paper. Satisfied that he was safe from detection, for he was a full league from the nearest British post, it is natural to suppose that he was happy in the thought that his perilous mission would soon be ended and that he was about to render to his honored commander-in-chief, Washington, and to his beloved country, the most valuable service yet attempted by any man in the American army. It was with these thoughts uppermost in his mind as he made his way to the landing that he made the fatal, error of his heroic and almost successful mission.

After his capture he was conveyed by the Halifax to New York City and taken to Howe's headquarters at Mount Pleasant, which was the elegant mansion of

Mr. James Beekman, on the East River, at the foot of the present Fifty-first Street, near First Avenue. Dr. Lossing, whom I have relied upon for information not easily obtainable from any other source, says: 'In 1849 I made a sketch of the Beekman mansion, and of the greenhouse in 1852, a few days before it was demolished, with all the glories of the garden. At the order of the street commissioner, streets were opened through the whole Beekman domain. The site of the greenhouse was in the center of what is now Fifty-second Street, a little east of First Avenue. It was erected in the spring of 1764. The mansion was occupied during the war as the headquarters of Generals Howe, Clinton and Robertson. It was the residence of the Brunswick General Riedesel and his family in the summer of 1780. General Carleton occupied it in 1783.''

At the time of Hale's capture and confinement in the greenhouse, the estate was deserted by its staunch Whig owner —James Beekman.

From the early descriptions given of the mansion and its surroundings it was unquestionably the finest estate in America prior to the Revolution. The greenhouse, that stood but a short distance from the dwelling, could not have been as "loathsome" as might be inferred from the writings of some over-zealous chroniclers, yet Paradise would have seemed a place of torment with Cunningham in authority.

Hale had been taken before Lord Howe late on the afternoon of Saturday, September 21st. When questioned he frankly admitted his name, his rank in the army and his mission as a spy, said a British officer afterward who was present at the "trial." He bitterly resented the accusation of being a traitor, and said that he had never looked upon King George as his sovereign, nor England as having any authority over the colonies. He did accept the brand of spy good-humoredly as he related his success in procuring valuable information in the British camps. He expressed regret that he had not been successful in delivering his information to Washington, and that he had not served his country better.

The additional evidence was the finding of the telltale papers in his shoes, which entitled him to a military trial according to the rules and usages of war. But this was denied him by Lord Howe, and he was immediately delivered into the custody of the infamous and brutal provost-marshal, William Cunningham. He was placed in the Beekman greenhouse under a strong guard "for execution at daybreak to-morrow." These were Howe's last words in the presence of Hale, but he gave detailed instructions to Cunningham as to when and how the execution should be conducted, and urged that all precautions be taken to prevent his escape.

General Howe, in the flush of his success, ignored the usages of war—to try men by court-martial before hanging them. So in the case of Nathan Hale, he decreed that the young patriot should die the death of a dog, without trial of any kind. Knowing the character of Cunningham, it was an unworthy, ungracious and altogether inhuman act to place a fellow-being in the clutches of so fiendish a creature as the notorious Cunningham. We must accept with a certain amount of allowance the testimony of an eyewitness to the meeting between Captain Hale and General Howe, when he says: "I observed that the frankness, the manly bearing and the evident, disinterested patriotism of the handsome young prisoner sensibly touched a tender chord of General Howe's nature; but the

stern rules of war concerning such
offences would not allow him to express
even pity." Had Howe wished to inflict
the worst torment possible he could not
have devised anything more brutal than
to have constituted himself judge and
jury, and after listening to the prisoner's
testimony, ordered him to be hanged before sunrise. It is no wonder that his
conscience troubled him in after years,
for we are told that when he had returned
to England, and after his retirement
from the army, his thoughts often re-
verted to scenes and events during the
American Revolution, but the hanging of
Nathan Hale without trial or the consolations of a spiritual adviser brought sorrow and grief to his last days.

Doomed as a spy—so young—so fair—
With fettered limbs and bosom bare,
He stood in the crisp autumn air
    Beneath the apple bough;

While 'round with taunt and ribald jest,
The British redcoats, gloating, pressed.
But heaven's bright sunshine crowned
    and kissed
  His calm, unruffled brow.

With patriot spirit kindling high,
And proud defiance in his eye,
To jibe and jeer he makes reply—
  (Such words forever live:)
"My sole regret as here I stand,
And wait the hangman's shameful hand,
Is that for my dear native land
  I've but one life to give."

    ·   ·   ·   ·   ·   ·   ·

The deed is done; his soul hath flown;
And lo! o'er Freedom's mountain throne
Another star in luster shone
  Adown the groves of time;
To cheer for aye the brave of heart,
Who spurn oppression's cruel smart,
And rise and rend their chains apart,
  In every race and clime.

And, oh, Columbia! mother mine—
Long may thy shield be freedom's sign,
Long may thy navies sweep the brine,
   Thine armies, hill and vale;
And when the war drums loudly peal,
Nor doubt nor danger can'st thou feel,
Bulwarked around by hearts of steel
   Like that of *Nathan Hale.*

CHAPTER VI.

"I REGRET THAT I HAVE BUT ONE POOR LIFE
TO LOSE FOR MY COUNTRY—IF I HAD
TEN THOUSAND LIVES I WOULD LAY
THEM DOWN, ONE AT A TIME, IN DE-
FENSE OF MY INJURED, BLEEDING
COUNTRY."

AT the same hour that Hale was lying
in the greenhouse awaiting his doom, the
lower part of the city was being de-
voured by flames; a fitting punishment
sent by Providence, the patriots thought,
to deprive their cruel oppressors of any
comforts the city might afford them during the long winter of 1776 and 1777.
Four hundred and ninety-three houses
were destroyed and fully one-third of
the population of the city, numbering

over twenty thousand, mostly Tories and British soldiers, were left without shelter and sufficient food, with an early winter just setting in.

The cause of the conflagration was attributed to the "rebel sympathizers," but subsequently it was found to have started in a low tavern on the wharf, now occupied by the Staten Island Ferry. The open fields to the south and the wide sweeping lawns and high terraces about the old mansion acted as a barrier to the fire's progress; but the heated atmosphere and dense smoke that reached the Beekman estate only irritated Cunningham the more and increased his hatred of Hale and his anxiety to hasten the execution.

Regardless of the fact that the morrow would be an autumn Sabbath in a Christian land, and having had his attention called to the impropriety of hanging a "criminal" on the "Lord's Day," Howe

dismissed the matter by saying that
the case was now in the hands of the
provost marshal. There is an abun-
dance of evidence to show the brutal
character of every man in authority sent
over by King George to force the Americans into submission, and the inhuman
Cunningham was only a tool in the hands
of his heartless master—Lord Howe.

During the early morning hours, Hale
requested the services of a minister,
which were refused him. He then asked
for a Bible, which was also denied him.
Two hours later he asked permission to
write to his mother and sweetheart, and
this would also have been refused, had not
a young British officer interfered and suggested that the letters, after inspection
by the provost marshal, could be sent
after Hale was executed. Being given a
candle and the necessary writing mate-
rials, Hale retired to send the last mes-
sage to those he loved; for already the

eastern sky showed faint evidences of the coming day, and when the bright sun should rise, his troubles, his part in the nation's struggles would be over.

One hour before sunrise the letters were handed Cunningham. Thinking they contained a further confession that would enable him to renew his persecutions, he hastily scanned their contents. When he observed the noble and patriotic spirit breathed in every word, every line, he grew furious and with his accustomed profane epithets, tore the letters into bits and stamped upon them before the victim of his wrath, announcing at the same time that the rebels should never know they had a man who could die with such firmness. Not one word of protest escaped the lips of Hale, who was resigned to his fate and seemed not to heed the insult or the impending scene that would witness the flight of his spirit from prison walls to the Elysian fields.

The place of execution has long been a subject of conjecture; some contending that it took place on the Beekman estate near where Hale was confined; others that he was executed at the barracks near Chambers Street, now the Hall of Records in the City Hall Park where all state criminals were executed, but the generally accepted location was in Colonel Rutger's orchard, whose mansion stood near the present junction of Pike and Monroe Streets, just back from the East River and not more than a mile from the Beekman estate.

The interview of Captain Wandell, as given in the opening chapter, would it seems, settle this much-mooted question, the importance of which is manifest, since the scene of his execution also fixes the location of his grave, now and for all time to come. Undisturbed for a century and a quarter, his mortal being now mingles with the soil for which he gave himself a willing sacrifice, while the influence of his martyrdom will endure forever in the hearts of his countrymen.

This testimony is further strengthened by Dr. Lossing who says: "In 1849 I visited the venerable Jeremiah Johnson, ex-mayor of Brooklyn, who was living at his farmhouse not far from the navy yard, then between the city of Brooklyn and the village of Williamsburg. Among other interesting facts concerning the Revolution of his own experience and observation which he had treasured in his memory was that his father was present at the execution of Captain Hale. Like other Long Island farmers at that time, he went to New York occasionally with truck. On the day of the great fire, he was there, when himself and team were pressed into the service of the British. He was with the detachment on Colonel Rutger's farm at the time of the execution and saw the martyr hanged upon the limb of an apple tree in Colonel Rutger's orchard. It was at the west side, not far from the line of (the present East Broadway."

Light was breaking in the east on that beautiful Sabbath morn of September 22, 1776, when Nathan Hale was led out for execution. Even at so early an hour as 5 A.M. a large number of men and women were present to witness the sad scene. Cunningham was there to give orders and evidently enjoyed the situation, for in a jocular and scoffing way he demanded of his victim his "last dying speech and confession." This did not call forth any resentful denunciation or emotional scene on the part of Hale. There on the threshold, on the border-land between life and death he stood beneath the apple bough a willing sacrifice for the cause and land he loved so well. Hear his last words as he fixes his gaze upon a multitude, among whom there was no friend to cheer him on his lonely journey across the dark river:

"Farewell: My only regret in dying is that I have but one poor life to lose for my country. If I had ten thousand lives I would lay them down one at a time in defense of my injured, bleeding country."

These were some of the sentiments contained in Hale's letter to his mother; what more he might have said was cut short by the cruel halter, for before the last word fell on that agitated throng, the fiend Cunningham shouted, "Swing him off!"

Where is it recorded in history that ever man died with such firmness, such devotion, such love of country? Yet Nathan Hale never saw the flag of the nation he gave his life to save.

The method employed at military executions was either to place a ladder against the tree, force the prisoner to ascend, place the rope about the neck, withdraw the ladder, leaving the victim suspended. Another way was to seat the condemned in a cart and after placing the noose about his neck, drive off, leaving the victim to strangle. History is silent as to which method was employed in the case of Captain Hale. Both seemed quite inhuman, for the victim is left to strangle in either method. We can be sure of one thing, however, and that is that Cunningham adopted the method that would produce the greatest amount of agony—prolonging the suffering for his own fiendish delight, and the gratification of a passion for witnessing human agony second only to the atrocities attributed to the Aztec priests in the performance of their religious rites, or the horrible saturnalia of Rome under the Cæsars.

It is quite proper to introduce a brief sketch of the fiend in whose charge Nathan Hale was placed, to see that Howe's orders were carried summarily into execution. Some authorities are averse to holding Howe responsible for the inhuman treatment Hale received during the few hours of his confinement, seeking a pretext in the unproved assertion that Cunningham was employed directly by the British ministry and was independent of the authority of Howe. However that may have been, it is known that Hale's captors took him before Howe, who, without advice or council pronounced his sentence and handed the prisoner over to Cunningham for execution. Howe, associated with General Clinton, was commander of the British forces in North America, while Cunningham was provost marshal for New York and Philadelphia only, and must have acted under the instructions of his chief—Lord William Howe.

Cunningham was described as a large,

burly, red-haired, red-faced Irishman, sixty years of age, excessively addicted to strong drink, and with most forbidding features. His cruelties and crimes committed while in charge of prisoners of war in New York were notorious and monstrous. Upon the scaffold in England, years after the war, he confessed that he had caused the death of fully two thousand prisoners under his charge, by starvation and otherwise. At times he put poison into the food and again he sold their rations, all for his own benefit, allowing the prisoners to starve.

A further account of Cunningham, one showing his low instincts and brutality, is given to illustrate the character of the men in authority who were striving to put down a rebellion which, if successful, meant our freedom and independence. " Wonted to sit in his quarters at the Provost, opposite the guard room on the right, and to drink punch till his brain was on fire—he would then stagger out into the corridors—followed often by his negro Richmond, the common hangman with coils of rope about his neck, and pouring forth volleys of tempestuous abuse on the wretched sufferers who happened to be outside their cells, drive the 'dogs,' as he called them, back to their 'kennels,' the 'rebel spawn,' as he varied it, 'into their holes'—or vent his spite, as he passed up and down the hall by kicking over vessels of soup which the charitable sometimes placed there for poor and friendless captives—or clanking his keys, reel to the door of the prison, and strain his drunken gaze for fresh victims."

The dreadful Weyler was moderate in his human sacrifices when compared with Cunningham, who is entitled to the distinction of being styled "The Modern Nero." We may derive some satisfaction from the story that his last years were passed in constant fear of death—despised, hated and shunned by everybody. He was finally strangled to death for a murder committed years before—a fitting end for one of earth's vilest and most atrocious characters.

．　．　．　．　．　．　．

Thus ended the life of the young patriot and martyr, Captain Nathan Hale. And while his brave mission resulted in failure so far as the objects he sought were concerned, he was successful in arousing the British to a realization of the fact that it was no easy task to conquer a people who were striving to throw off the yoke of tyranny and oppression that had driven their Old-World ancestors to acts of desperation and kept all Europe in insurrection and revolution for a thousand years. The privations and dangers they encountered in the New World only whetted their ambition to build anew a republic that would permit neither idiotic king nor debased soldiery to make their laws, nor to aid in their enforcement. It also showed the British that the patriot army, numbering nearly fourteen thousand, contained few men who would not sacrifice everything for the cause of liberty and independence.

The death of Nathan Hale was a sad blow to all of his friends and acquaintances, but to none more especially than to Alice Adams, his betrothed. Her constant solicitude concerning his dangerous occupation, her devotion that became a part of her life and religion were almost as pathetic as his ignominious death and burial in an unknown grave. After Nathan's death she married Eleazer Ripley, who left her a widow in less than a year. Subsequently she married William Lawrence of Hartford, Connecticutt, where she lived until her death in September, 1845. Her last words were, "Write to Nathan!"

STATUE OF NATHAN HALE IN CITY HALL PARK, NEW YORK.

Shortly after Hale's death a ballad
was written which was very popular
during the remaining years of the war.
It was altered slightly and again became popular during the second war with
Great Britain in 1812. It was evidently
written by one who was not well in-
formed as to all the details concerning
Hale's mission, capture and execution:

The breezes went steadily through the
    tall pines,
  A-saying "Oh, hush!" a-saying "Oh,
    hush!"
As stilly stole by a bold legion of horse,
  For Hale's in the bush, for Hale's in
    the bush.
"Keep still!" said the thrush, as she
    nestled her young
  In a nest by the road, in a nest by the
    road.

"For the tyrants are near, and with them
     appear
  What bodes us no good, what bodes
     us no good."

The brave captain heard it, and thought
     of his home,
  In a cot by the brook, in a cot by the
     brook,
With mother and sister, and memories
     dear,
  He so gayly forsook, he so gayly for-
     sook.

Cooling shades of the night were coming
     apace.
  The tattoo had beat, the tattoo had
     beat.
The noble one sprang from his dark hid-
     ing-place,
  To make his retreat, to make his re-
     treat.

He wearily trod on the dry rustling
    leaves,
    As he passed through the wood, as he
        passed through the wood,
And silently gained his rude launch on
    the shore,
    As she played with the flood, as she
        played with the flood.

The guards of the camp, on that dark,
    dreary night,
    Had a murderous will, had a murder-
        ous will.
They took him, and bore him afar from
    the shore,
    To a hut on the hill, to a hut on the
        hill.

No mother was there, nor a friend who
    could cheer,
    In that little stone cell, in that little
        stone cell.

But he trusted in love from his Father
above.
In his heart all was well, in his heart
all was well.

An ominous owl, with his solemn bass
voice,
Sat moaning hard by, sat moaning
hard by:
"The tyrant's proud minions must
gladly rejoice,
For he must soon die, for he must
soon die."

The brave fellow faced them, no thing
he restrained,
The cruel gen'ral, the cruel gen'ral:
His errand from camp, of the ends to be
gained,
And said that was all, and said that
was all.

They took him, and bound him, and
    bore him away,
  Down the hill's grassy side, down the
    hill's grassy side.
'Twas there the base hirelings in royal
    array
  His cause did deride, his cause did
    deride.

Five minutes were given, short minutes,
    no more,
  For him to repent, for him to repent.
He prayed for his mother, he asked not
    another,
  To heaven he went, to heaven he went.

The faith of a martyr the tragedy
    showed,
As he trod the last stage, as he trod the
    last stage.
And Britons will shudder at gallant
    Hale's blood,
  As his words do presage, as his
    words do presage.

Thou pale king of terrors, thou life's
    gloomy foe,
  Go frighten the slave, go frighten the
      slave;
Tell tyrants to you their allegiance they
    owe.
  No fears for the brave, no fears for the
      brave!

CHAPTER VII.

"Ye come with hearts that oft have glowed
    At his soul-stirring tale,
To wreath the deathless evergreen
    Around the name of HALE."

THE career of Nathan Hale has been compared with that of John André, a major in the British army. Both were young, both were spies and both were publicly executed for an offense not sanctioned by civilized nations. In character, and the spirit in which they served their respective countries, they differed widely; Hale was a patriot of the highest type, while André was an adventurer in the service of a tyrannical king.

The occupation of a spy is honorable only when the service is performed unselfishly for one's country—without hope or expectation of personal reward of any kind; this was the case with Nathan Hale, whose last words on the scaffold were: "If I had ten thousand lives I would lay them down, one at a time, in defense of my injured, bleeding country." The occupation of a spy, when the service is rendered with this spirit, is just as honorable as was the act of Washington when he left his camp fires burning at the battle of Trenton, "to *deceive* the enemy."

Contrast the last words of Major André, who said: "I request you, gentlemen, that you will bear me witness to the world, that I die like a brave man." He avowedly admitted that in the enterprise that resulted in his capture and execution that he "sought military glory, the applause of his king and perhaps a brigadiership should success crown his efforts as a spy."

Howe had decreed that Hale should

"die like a dog" and his instructions
were faithfully followed; for during the
twenty-two hours of his imprisonment
he was not given a particle of food and
but two cups of water, which doubtless,
Cunningham would have poisoned had he
not believed that the halter was the
surer and more humiliating method, and
that in the present instance he was acting under instructions from Lord Howe.
André, on the other hand, was shown
every kindness, was provided with
counsel, given every opportunity to prove
his innocence, and was fed from Washington's private table. Dr. Depew has
given us a character-portrait of both
Hale and André and his estimate of
each. There is no doubt that Dr. Depew
has expressed the sentiment of his countrymen as regards the character of these
martyrs of the American Revolution, and
this comparison of the two men is
given in the final chapter of this book.

Although four generations have come and gone since the life drama of Nathan Hale was enacted, it is gratifying to know that men are awakening to a full sense of the importance of the mission of that young patriot and martyr. Public sentiment has been aroused and today the name of Hale stands forth as the bright and shining light during the dark days of the nation's struggle for independence. No marble shaft nor modest stone marks the resting-place of the martyr, and for more than half a century after his death no effort was made to perpetuate his memory, in bronze or granite. Even the spot is unknown where sleeps this hero and martyr of the Revolution.

In destroying the life of the young patriot, the British sought to bury forever the name and deeds of Captain Hale, but in this they were unsuccessful, for on the 25th of November, 1837—sixty-one years and two months after Hale's death, twenty revolutionary soldiers, hale and hearty in their fourscore years, met at a banquet in Coventry, Connecticut, and formed the "Hale Monument Association." Many efforts were made to induce Congress to make a suitable appropriation for so worthy a cause, but all efforts failed, notwithstanding attention had been called to the honor England had shown André, by erecting a grand mausoleum over his remains in Westminster Abbey.

"The Hale Monument Association" determined that their initial effort should not be in vain. For the purpose of securing funds, a series of festivals was determined upon, in the nature of church fairs, tea parties, public entertainments, private readings, and at all times "private contributions were gladly accepted." In these and in many other ways the people of Connecticut almost unconsciously aided in raising a goodly sum. It was a strange way to raise money for a monument, but desperate and heroic measures are sometimes necessary when other and more appropriate means are wanting. At one of these fairs held in the Congregational Church at New Haven, December 10, 1839, a poem was addressed to "The Daughters of Freedom" and printed on white satin, which sold readily at fifty cents apiece. It contained the following verses:

" *Ye come with hearts that oft have glowed*
    At his soul-stirring tale,
To wreath the deathless evergreen
    Around the name of HALE.

"Here his memorial stone shall rise
    In freedom's hallowed shade,
Prouder than André's trophied tomb,
    'Mid mightiest monarchs laid."

In 1845 the State of Connecticut ap-

propriated twelve hundred and fifty dollars, and this, together with the twenty-
five hundred dollars contributed by the
patriotic citizens of Coventry and vicinity and the sum raised by entertainments, gave the "Hale Monument Association" three thousand seven hundred
and fifty dollars with which to erect a
suitable monument which should be "a
substantial testimony to Hale's memory." Henry Austin of New Haven designed the monument, which was con-
structed under the supervision of Solo-
mon Willard, the architect of the Bunker
Hill Monument. The Hale memorial at
Coventry was unveiled in the summer of
1846. It stands upon a pleasant elevation near the old Congregational Church
where Hale was baptized more than a
half-century before. The beautiful
Waugumbaug Lake, where Hale was
wont to skate and fish when a boy,
glistens in the distance. This column of

Quincy granite is forty-five feet high and fourteen and a half feet square at its base. Each side of the pedestal bears an inscription. On the north side facing Lake Waugumbaug is chiseled:

"CAPTAIN NATHAN HALE.'

On the west side:

"BORN AT CONVENTRY, JUNE 6, 1755."

On the east side: .

"DIED AT NEW YORK, SEPTEMBER 22, 1776."

On the south side:

"I regret that I have but one life to lose for my country."

This was the first monument erected to the memory of Nathan Hale, though it must not be forgotten that, during the second war with Great Britain in 1812, a little fort that was erected during the Revolution at the entrance to New Haven harbor was named "Fort Hale" in honor of the first martyr of the Revolution.

In June, 1887, a magnificent life-size bronze statue of Hale was placed in the rotunda of the State Capitol at Hartford, Connecticut, at the expense of the State. This statue was the work of Karl Gerhardt, and the presentation address was delivered by Charles Dudley Warner, with response and address of acceptance by Governor Phineas Lounsbury.

There seemed to be great activity among the descendants of the Revolutionary patriots at about this time to perpetuate the memory of the brave young martyr. Poems and brief sketches of the services he rendered Washington began to make their appearance, and on the 25th of November, 1893, just fifty-six years after the forming of the "Hale Monument Association" at Coventry, and one hundred and ten years after the evacuation of New York by the British, a magnificent bronze statue of heroic size was unveiled at the City Hall Park,

New York City, under the auspices of
"The Sons of the Revolution." Ten
thousand people were present at the unveiling of the statue which was executed
by the sculptor, MacMonnies. A civil
and military parade preceded the exer-
cises. Many of the public buildings in
New York and Brooklyn were draped in
bunting; the cities put on their gala day
attire, and amid the booming of cannon
and songs that stirred the vast multitude, a monument befitting the name
and deeds of the young martyr was unveiled in the presence of many thousands,
in the vicinity where he performed his
daring mission and paid the penalty of
his misfortune.

Although few biographies of Captain
Hale have appeared, yet his life has been
rendered familiar to millions by numer-
ous poetic effusions which have appeared
at intervals during the passing century. The chief purpose of the author

NATHAN HALE MONUMENT, SOUTH COVENTRY, CONN.

Chiseled upon the monument are the following inscriptions :—

CAPTAIN NATHAN HALE,
1776.
Born at Coventry,
June 6, 1755.
Died at New York,
Sept. 22, 1776.

"I only regret that I have but one life to lose for my country."

has been to gather each scrap of tribute to the memory of the brave youth, that future generations may know the spirit of the men who defied British power and arrogance at a time when her supremacy was unquestioned on both hemispheres.

A short time after Hale's death a personal friend of the martyr wrote a poem, too lengthy to be reproduced here, in which he described the personal appearance of Nathan Hale and his motives in becoming a spy. The name of the author was not affixed to the original production, and consequently the authorship of the following poetic tribute must forever remain unknown:

Removed from envy, malice, pride and
    strife,
He walked through goodness as he
    walked through life;
A kinder brother Nature never knew,
A child more duteous or a friend more
    true.

Hate of oppression's arbitrary plan,
The love of freedom and the rights of
   man;
A strong desire to save from slavery's
   chain
The future millions of the western main.

Not Socrates nor noble Russell died,
Or gentle Sidney, Britain's boast and
   pride,
Or gen'rous Moore, approached life's
   final goal
With more composed, more firm and
   stable soul.

Dr. Timothy Dwight, who was one of
Hale's tutors during the two years he
spent at Yale College, said at his graduation: "Yale has never graduated a
more promising class." Then turning
to Hale, he added, "And to you, Mr. Hale,
the youngest who ever went out from
these classic halls, I predict a glorious

future and a sublime mission in life."
Though his future was brief it was
indeed glorious. Could a prophecy have
been more accurately foretold?

In one of the catalogues of Yale College, issued during the presidency of that
great and good man, Dr. Dwight, there
appeared a brief tribute to Nathan Hale
over the signature of one of Yale's most
illustrious presidents. It is brief and
runs:

Thus while fond Virtue wished in vain to
    save,
HALE, bright and generous, found a
    hapless grave;
With genius' living flame his bosom
    glowed,
And Science lured him to her sweet
    abode.
In Worth's fair path his feet adventured
    far,
The pride of peace, the rising hope of
    war;

In duty firm, in danger calm and even,
To friends unchanging and sincere to
    Heaven.
How short his course, the prize how early
    won!
While weeping Friendship mourns her
    favorite son.

Mr. John S. Babcock, for many years
a resident of Coventry, and a poet having
more than a local reputation, wrote a
touching tribute to Hale's memory,
which appeared first in the papers of
his native city. Mr. Babcock wrote in
the strain of Charles Wolfe's "The
Burial of Sir John Moore." The
rhythmic meter of that famous poem has
been faithfully reproduced in these two
stanzas:

He fell in the spring of his early prime,
  With his fair hopes all around him;

He died for his birth-land—a glorious
    crime,
  Ere the palm of his fame had crowned
    him.

He fell in her darkness, he lived not to
    see
  The morn of her risen glory;
But the name of the brave, in the heart
    of the free,
  Shall be twined in her deathless story.

Timothy Dwight was an intimate friend
of Hale and the year after the martyr's
death he entered the Continental army
as chaplain of the regiment to which
Hale belonged. The following poem was
written in 1777 and inscribed to Nathan
Hale. It was first published in "Kettell's Specimens," in 1829:

To Nathan Hale:

COLUMBIA.

BY TIMOTHY DWIGHT.

Columbia, Columbia, to glory arise,
The queen of the world, and child of the
    skies;
Thy genius commands thee, with rapture
    behold,
While ages on ages thy splendor unfold;
Thy reign is the last, and the noblest of
    time,
Most fruitful thy soil, most inviting thy
    clime;
Let the crimes of the East ne'er encrim-
    son thy name,
Be freedom and silence and virtue thy
    fame.

To conquest and slaughter let Europe
    aspire;
Whelm nations in blood and wrap cities
    in fire;

Thy heroes the rights of mankind shall
    defend
And triumph pursue them, and glory
    attend,
A world in thy realm: for a world be
    thy laws,
Enlarged as thine empire and just as thy
    cause;
On freedom's broad basis, that empire
    shall rise,
Extend with the main, and dissolve with
    the skies.

Fair science her gates to thy sons shall
    nbar,
And the East see the morn hide the
    beams of her star.
New bards and new sages, unrivalled
    shall soar
To fame unextinguished, when time is
    no more;
To thee, the last refuge of virtue de-
    signed,

Shall fly from all nations the best of
    mankind;
Here, grateful to heaven, with transport
    shall bring,
Their incense, more fragrant than odors
    of Spring.

Nor less shall thy fair ones to glory
    ascend,
And genius and beauty in harmony
    blend;
The graces of form shall awake pure de-
    sire,
And the charms of the soul ever cherish
    the fire;

Their sweetness unmingled, their man-
    ners refined,
And virtue's bright image, instamped on
    the mind,
With peace and soft rapture shall teach
    life to glow,
And light up a smile in the aspect of woe.

Thy fleets to all regions, thy power shall
    display,
The nations admire and the oceans obey;
Each shore to thy glory its tribute unfold,
And the East and the South yield their
    spices and gold.
As the day-spring unbounded, **thy**
    splendor shall flow,
And earth's little kingdoms before thee
    shall bow;
While the ensigns of union, in triumph
    unfurled,
Hush the tumult of war and give peace
    to the world.

Thus, as down a lone valley, with cedars
    o'erspread,
From war's dread confusion I pensively
    strayed,
The gloom from the face of fair heaven
    retired;
The winds ceased to murmur; the thun-
    ders expired;

Perfumes of Eden flowed sweetly along,
And a voice as of angels, enchantingly
    sung:
Columbia, Columbia, to glory arise,
The queen of the world, and the child of
    the skies.

CHAPTER VIII.

CONCLUSION—EULOGIUMS.

ANDRE's story is the one overmastering romance of the Revolution. American and English literature is full of eloquence and poetry in tribute to his memory and sympathy for his fate. After the lapse of a hundred years there is no abatement of absorbing interest. What had this young man done to merit immortality? The mission, whose tragic issue lifted him out of the oblivion of other minor British officers, in its inception was free from peril or daring, and its objects and purposes were utterly infamous. Had he succeeded by the desecration of the honorable uses of passes and flags of truce, his name would have

been held in everlasting execration. In
his failure, the infant Republic escaped
the dagger with which he was feeling for
its heart, and the crime was drowned in
tears for his untimely end. His youth
and beauty, his skill with pen and pencil,
the brightness of his life, the calm courage in the gloom of his death, his early
love and disappointment, surrounded
him with a halo of poetry and pity which
secured for him what he most sought
and could never have won in battle and
sieges—a fame and recognition which
have outlived that of all the generals
under whom he served.

Are kings only grateful, and do re-
publics forget? Is fame a travesty, and
the judgment of mankind a farce?
America had a parallel case in Captain
Nathan Hale. Of the same age as
André, he graduated at Yale College
with high honors, enlisted in the patriot
cause at the beginning of the contest,

and secured the love and confidence of all about him. When none else would go upon a most important and perilous mission he volunteered, and was captured by the British. While André received every kindness, courtesy and attention, and was fed from Washington's table, Hale was thrust into a noisome dungeon in the sugar house. While André was tried by a board of officers and had ample time and every facility for defense, Hale was summarily ordered to execution the next morning. While André's last wishes and behests were sacredly followed, the infamous Cunningham tore from Hale his cherished Bible and destroyed before his eyes his last letters to his mother and sisters, and asked him what he had to say. "All I have to say," was his reply, "is, I regret I have but one life to lose for my country." His death was concealed for months because Cunningham said he did not want the rebels to know they had a man who could die so bravely. And yet while André rests in that grandest of mausoleums, where the proudest of nations garners the remains and perpetuates the memories of its most eminent and honored children, the name and deeds of Nathan Hale have passed into oblivion.

This tribute from one of America's foremost orators, Chauncey M. Depew, is striking in its brevity and well-chosen words. The address was delivered by Dr. Depew nearly twenty years ago, and like that of Mr. Raymond and the poetic tribute of Isaac Hinton Brown, had much to do with the revival of interest in the name and deeds of the young martyr, and made the unveiling of two monuments to his memory a nation's rejoicing.

At an early stage of the Revolution, Nathan Hale, captain in the American

army, which he had entered, abandoning
brilliant prospects of professional distinction for the sole purpose of defending the liberties of his country—gifted,
educated, ambitious—the equal of André
in talent, in worth, in amiable manners,
and in every manly quality, and his
superior in that final test of character—
the motives by which his acts were
prompted and his life was guided—laid
aside every consideration personal to
himself and entered upon a service of
infinite hazard to life and honor, because
Washington deemed it important to the
sacred cause to which both had been
sacredly set apart. Like André, he was
found in the hostile camp; like him,
though without trial, he was adjudged
as a spy; and, like him, he was condemned to death.

And here the likeness ends. No con-
soling word, no pitying or respectful
look, cheered the dark hours of his

doom.   He was met with insult at every turn.   The sacred consolations of the minister of God were denied him; the Bible was taken from him; with an excess of barbarity hard to be paralleled in civilized war, his dying letters of farewell to his mother and sisters were destroyed in his presence; and uncheered by sympathy, mocked by brutal power, and attended only by that sense of duty, incorruptible, undefiled, which had ruled his life—finding a fit farewell in the serene and sublime regret that he had but one life to lose for his country—he went forth to meet the great darkness of an ignominious death.

The loving hearts of his early companions have erected a neat monument to his memory in his native town; but, beyond that little circle, where stands his name recorded?   While the majesty of England, in the person of her sovereign, sent an embassy across the sea to solicit the remains of André at the hands of his foes, that they might be enshrined in that sepulcher where she garners the relics of her mighty and renowned sons— "Splendid in their ashes, pompous in the grave," the children of Washington have left the body of Nathan Hale to sleep in its unknown tomb, though it be on his native soil, unhonored by any outward observance, unmarked by any memorial stone. Monody, eulogy, monument of marble or of brass and of letters more enduring than all, have in his own land and in ours given the name and fate of André to the sorrowing remembrance of all time to come. American genius has celebrated his praises, has sung his virtues, and exalted to heroic heights his prayer, manly, but personal to himself, for choice in the manner of death—his dying challenge to all men to witness the courage with which he met his fate. But where, save on the cold page of history, stands the record of Captain Nathan Hale? Where is the hymn that speaks to immortality, and tells of the added brightness and enhanced glory when his soul joined its noble host? And where sleeps the American of Americans that their hearts are not stirred to solemn means of rapture at the thought of the sublime love of country which buoyed him not alone above the fear of death, but far beyond all thought of himself, of his fate and his fame, or of anything less than his country—and which shaped his dying breath into the sacred sentence which trembled at the last upon his quivering lip?

These eloquent words had a deeper significance when they were uttered by Mr. Raymond more than half a century ago than they have today, for the patriotic spirit that runs high in the breast of every American has arisen to the occasion and necessity of recognizing the services Nathan Hale rendered the "Father of His Country."

It is a just reproach to a nation of nearly sixty million freemen, rich and powerful beyond any other people on the globe, that the memory of Nathan Hale, their self-sacrificing benefactor in purpose, and a true and noble martyr in the cause of the liberty they enjoy, has been, until lately, absolutely neglected by them; that no monody, eulogy, monument of marble or of brass, dedicated to him by the public voice, appears anywhere in our broad land. Let the conscience of our people, inspired by gratitude and patriotism, be fairly awakened to the propriety of the undertaking, and the funds will speedily be forthcoming sufficient to erect a magnificent monument in memory of Nathan Hale in the city where he died for his country. I recommended, as a portion of the inscription upon the monument, the subjoined epitaph, written fully thirty years ago by George Gibbs, the ripe scholar and antiquary, who was at one time the librarian of the New York Historical Society:

Stranger, Beneath this Stone
Lies the Dust of
a Spy
Who Perished Upon the Gibbet;
Yet
The Storied Marbles of the Great
The Shrines of Heroes,
Entombed not one more Worthy of
Honor
Than him who here
Sleeps his last sleep.
Nations
Bow with Reverence before the Dust
Of him who dies
A glorious death,
Urged on by the Sound of the
Trumpet
And the shouts of
Admiring thousands.
But what Reverence, what honor,
Is not due to one
Who for his country encountered
Even an infamous death,
Soothed by no sympathy,
Animated by no praise!

—BENSON J. LOSSING.

Washington Irving, in his "Life of George Washington," recites an interesting story of the capture of André by Major Tallmadge near Tappan, where Tallmadge informs the British spy, when questioned as to his probable fate, that it will be similar to that of the American spy, Captain Nathan Hale—seven years before.

After disembarking at King's Ferry near Stony Point, they set off for Tappan under escort of a body of horse. As they approached the Clove, a deep defile in the rear of the Highlands, André, who rode beside Tallmadge, became solicitous to know the opinion of the latter as to what would be the result of his capture, and in what light he would be regarded by General Washington and by a military tribunal, should one be ordered. Tallmadge evaded the question as long as possible, but being urged to a full and explicit reply, gave it, he says, in the following words:

"I had a much-loved classmate in Yale College, by the name of Nathan Hale, who entered the army in 1775. Immediately after the battle of Long Island, General Washington wanted information respecting the strength, position and probable movements of the enemy. Captain Hale tendered his services, went over to Brooklyn and was taken, just as he was passing the outposts of the enemy on his return; said I with emphasis—do you remember the sequel of the story? 'Yes,' said André. 'He was hanged as a spy. But you surely do not consider his case and mine alike?' 'Yes, precisely similar, and similar will be your fate.'"

Here Washington Irving recites the brief story of Nathan Hale and his unsuccessful mission. It is in brief what this book aims to give in detail. The story of Nathan Hale cannot be too often told, for it is the best illustration we have of the character of the men we owe a debt that neither this nor all future generations can hope to repay.

In comparing the mission of the two men—André and Hale—the fate of each, and the action England took with regard to the remains and memory of André, Henry Cabot Lodge says:

"André was a spy and briber, who sought to ruin the American cause by the treachery of an American general. It was a dark and dangerous game, and he knew that he staked his life on the result. He failed, and paid the penalty. Washington could not permit, he would have been grossly and feebly culpable if he had permitted such an attempt to pass without extreme punishment. He was generous and magnanimous, but he was not a sentimentalist, and he punished this miserable treason, so far as he could reach it, as it deserved. It is true that André was a man of talent, well-bred and courageous, and of engaging manners. He deserved all the sympathy and sorrow which he excited at the time, but nothing more. He was not only technically a spy, but he had sought his ends by bribery, he had prostituted a flag of truce, and he was to be richly paid for his work. It was all hire and salary. No doubt André was patriotic and loyal. Many spies have been the same, and have engaged in their dangerous exploits from the highest motives. Nathan Hale, whom the British hanged without compunction, was as well-born and well-bred as André, and as patriotic as man could be, and moreover he was a spy and nothing more. André was a trafficker in bribes and treachery, and however we may pity his fate, his name has no proper place in the great temple at Westminster, where all English-speaking people bow with reverence, and only a most perverted sentimentality could conceive that it was fitting to erect

a monument to his memory in this
country.''

NATHAN HALE, THE MARTYR SPY.

'Twas in the year that gave the nation
    birth—
A time when men esteemed the common
    good
As greater weal than private gain. A
    battle fierce
And obstinate had laid a thousand pat-
    riots low,
And filled the people's hearts with gloom.

Pursued like hunted deer,
The crippled army fled; and, yet, amid
Disaster and defeat, the nation's chosen
    chief
Resolved his losses to retrieve. But not
With armies disciplined and trained by
    years
Of martial service, could he, this Fabian
    chief,

Now hope to check the hosts of Howe's
    victorious legions—
These had he not.

  In stratagem the shrewder general
Ofttimes o'ercomes his strong antag-
    onist.
To Washingon a knowledge of the plans,
Position, strength of England's force
Must compensate for lack of numbers.

  He casts about for one who'd take his
    life
In hand. Lo! he stands before the chief.
    In face,
A boy—in form, a man on whom the eye
    could rest
In search of God's perfected handiwork.
In culture, grace and speech, reflecting
    all
A mother's love could lavish on an only
    son.

The chieftain's keen discerning eye
Appraised the youth at his full worth,
    and saw
In him those blending qualities that make
The hero and the sage. He fain would
    save
For nobler deeds a man whose presence
    marked
A spirit born to lead.

"Young man," he said with kindly air,
"Your country and commander feel
    grateful that
Such talents are offered in this darkening
    hour.
Have you in reaching this resolve, con-
    sidered well
Your fitness, courage, strength—the act,
    the risk
You undertake? Have you, in that fine
    balance, which
Detects an atom on either beam, weighed
    well

Your chances of escape 'gainst certain
     fate
Should capture follow in the British
     camp?''

In tones of fitting modesty that well
Became his years, the patriot answered
     thus:
"My country's honor, safety, life, it ever
     was
My highest purpose to defend: that
     country's foes
Exultant sweep through ruined land and
     home
And field. A thousand stricken hearts
     bewail
The loss of those who late our standards
     bore
Appeals to us through weeping eyes
     whose tears
We cannot brush away with words. The
     ranks

Of those now cold in death are not re-
    placed
By living men. The hour demands a
    duty rare—
Perhaps a sacrifice. If God and training in
The schools have given me capacities
This duty to perform, the danger of the
    enterprise
Should not deter me from the act
Whose issue makes our country free. In
    times
Like these a nation's life sometimes upon
A single life depends. If mine be deemed
A fitting sacrifice, God grant a quick
Deliverance."

"Enough, go then, at once," the great
Commander said. "May heaven's guard-
    ian angel give
You safe return. Adieu."

Disguised with care, the hopeful cap-
    tain crossed

The Sound, and moved through British
     camp
Without discovery by troops or refugees.
The enemy's full strength, in men, in
     stores,
Munitions, guns—all military accoutre-
     ments
Were noted with exact precision; while
With graphic sketch, each trench and
     parapet,
Casemated battery, magazine and every
     point
Strategic, was drawn with artist's skill.

    The task complete, the spy with heart
Elate, now sought an exit through the
     lines.
Well might he feel a soldier's pride. An
     hour hence
A waiting boat would bear him to his
     friends.
His plans he'd lay before his honored
     chief;

His single hand might turn the tide of
  war,
His country yet be free.

"Halt!" a British musket leveled at
His head dimmed all the visions of his
  soul.
A dash—an aimless shot; the spy bore
  down
Upon the picket with a blow that else
Had freed him from his clutch, but for a
  score
Of troopers stationed near. In vain he
  struggles fierce
And desperate—in vain demands to be
  released.
A Tory relative, for safety quartered in
The British camp, would prove his
  truckling loyalty
With kinsman's blood. A word—a look—
A motion of the head, and he who'd
  dared

So much in freedom's name was free no
   more.

Oh, Judas, self condemned! thou art
But the type of many a trait'rous friend,
Who ere and since thy time betrayed to
   death
A noble heart. Henceforth be doubly
   doomed—
A base example to earth's weaker souls.

Before Lord Howe the captive youth
Was led. "Base dog!" the haughty
   general said,
"Ignoble son of loyal sires! you've
   played the spy
Quite well, I ween. The cunning skill
   wherewith
You wrought these plans and charts
   might well adorn
An honest man; but in a rebel's hands
   they're vile
And mischievous. If aught may palliate

A traitor's act, attempted in his sover-
    eign's camp,
I bid you speak ere I pronounce your
    sentence."

With tone and mien that hushed
The buzzing noise of idle lackeys in the
    hall,
The patriot thus replied: "You know
    my name—
My rank—my treach'rous kinsman made
My purpose plain. I've nothing further
    of myself
To tell beyond the charge of traitor to
    deny.
The brand of spy I do accept without re-
    proach;
But never since I've known the base in-
    gratitude
Of king to loyal subjects of his realm
Has British rule been aught to me than
    barbarous

Despotism which God and man abhor,
    and none
But dastards fear to overthrow.

"For tyrant royalty your lordship
    represents
I never breathed a loyal breath; and he
Who calls me traitor seeks a pretext for
    a crime
His trembling soul might well condemn."

"I'll hear no more such prating cant,"
Said Howe, "your crime's enough to
    hang a dozen men.
Before tomorrow's sun comes up you'll
    swing
'Twixt earth and heaven, that your
    countrymen
May know a British camp is dangerous
    ground
For prowling spies.   Away."

In loathsome cell, derived
Of holy sacrament, and e'en the word of
    Him
Who cheered the thief upon the cross—
    refused
The means wherewith he would indite
    his last
Farewell to her who gave him life,
And to another whose young heart
The morrow's work would shade in
    gloom,
He passed the night in charge of one
    who Satan had
Commissioned hell's sharpest torments
    to inflict.

.   .   .   .

Securely bound upon a cart, amid
A speechless crowd, he stands beneath a
    strong
Projecting limb, to which a rope with
    noose attached

Portends a tragic scene. He casts his
    eyes
Upon the surging multitude. Clearly
    now
His tones ring out as victors shout in
    triumph:

"Men, I do not die in vain,
My humble death upon this tree will
    light anew
The Torch of Liberty. A hundred hands
    to one
Before will strike for country, home and
    God,
And fill our ranks with men of faith in
    His
Eternal plan to make this people free.
A million prayers go up this day to free
The land from blighting curse of tyrant's
    rule.
Oppression's wrongs have reached Je-
    hovah's throne:

The God of vengeance smites the foe!
    This land—
This glorious land—is free—is free!
My friends, farewell!   In dying thus
I feel but one regret; it is the one poor
    life
I have to give in Freedom's cause."
          —ISAAC HINTON BROWN.

THE END.

www.ingramcontent.com/pod-product-compliance
Lightning Source LLC
Chambersburg PA
CBHW021117020726
47500CB00003B/794